characters created by

lauren child

Look after YOUR Planet

PUFFIN

Charlie ♥ and Lola™

written by Bridget Hurst

Text based on the script

produced by Tiger Aspect

Illustrations from the TV animation

PUFFIN BOOKS
Published by the Penguin Group: London, New York, Australia,
Canada, India, Ireland, New Zealand and South Africa
Penguin Books Ltd, Registered Offices: 80 Strand, London WC2R 0RL, England

puffinbooks.com

First published 2008
This edition published 2011
006
Text and illustrations copyright © Lauren Child/Tiger Aspect Productions Limited, 2008
The Charlie and Lola logo is a trademark of Lauren Child
ISBN: 978-0-141-33373-1

Printed on 128gsm Matt Art Sun FSC™ paper in China

MIX
Paper from
responsible sources
FSC™ C018179

I have this little sister Lola.
She is small and very funny.
    Lola loves keeping things. All kinds of things.
Boxes, old broken toys... just things.

"Not any more!"
    says Lola.

I say,
"Has it got **anything**
        to do with when
we went to Marv's house?"

And Lola says,
        "Mmm, maybe..."

Yesterday, Marv said,
"I dare **anyone** to go into my
big brother Marty's room.
He doesn't let anyone touch any of his things
and he won't **throw anything** away.
Mum says his room looks like
a **complete** pigsty."

I say, "He can't be that bad."

When we sneak into
Marty's bedroom,
Lola says,
    "Ooh, it's pongy."

But then we hear,
"Get out
    of my
    room!
    ... NOW!!"

And Marv shouts,
    "Run!"

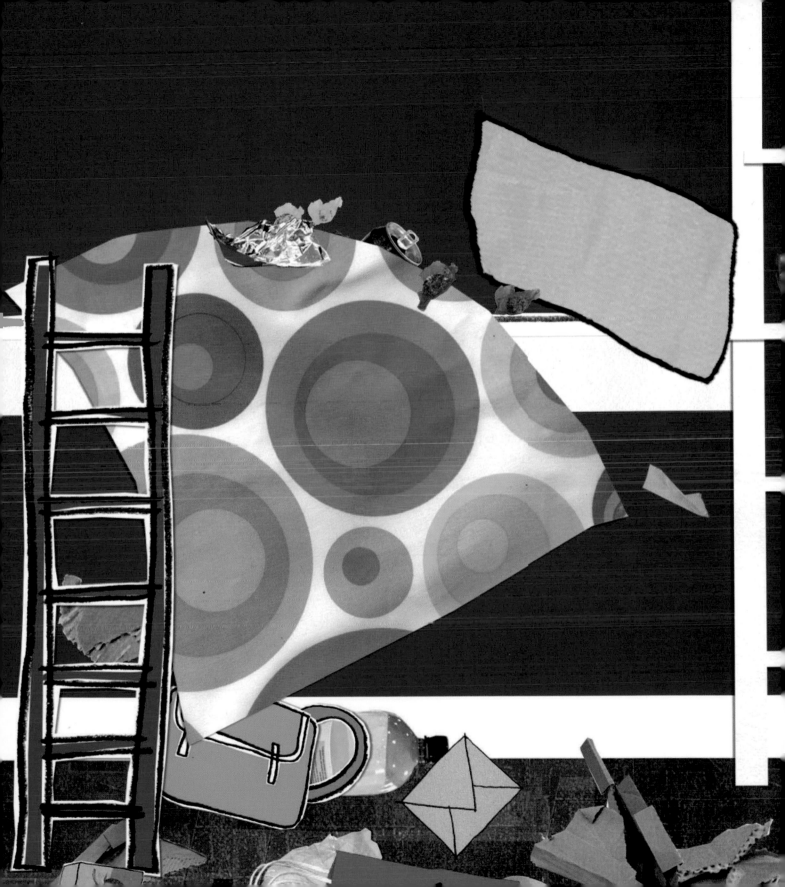

"So you see, Charlie,
        I do not ever, never want my room to look
like Marty's. So I am throwing everything away.
        Because I do not need it."

"Why don't you recycle it?"

And Lola says,
        "Bicycle it?"

"No, **re-cycle** it."

"**Recycle** it? What is that?" says Lola.

"Well, it's a way
that people can **reuse**
OLD things in a different
and NEW-ish way."

"Why?" says Lola.

"Because if we **throw** everything away, then we will all be **completely** buried under a

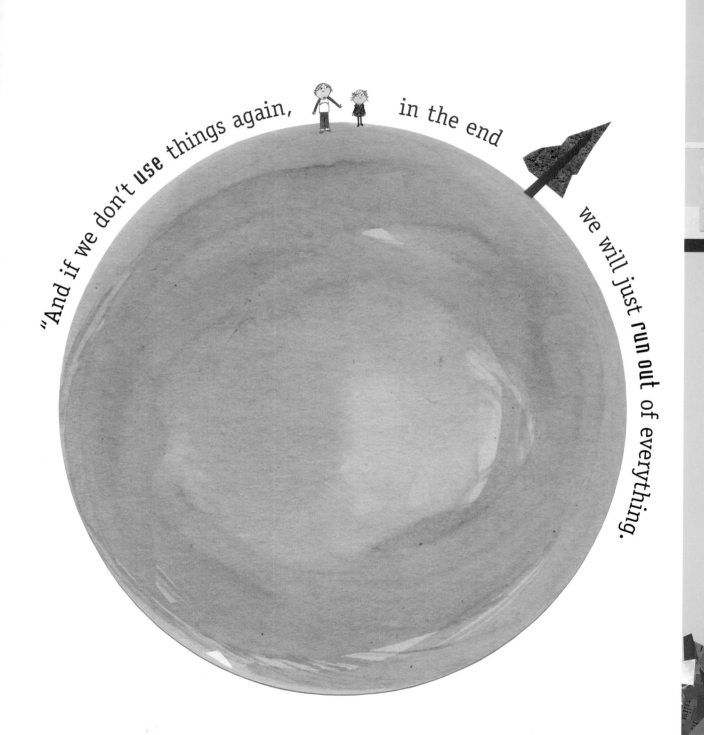

"And if we don't **use** things again, in the end we will just **run out** of everything.

So **recycling** is a good thing.

Did you know there are
these places where they make
NEW paper out of OLD paper.

The OLD paper gets
squidged up with
water and things.

And then they
press it all flat.

"Then they make
all sorts of NEW
types of paper, like…

writing
paper,

toilet paper,

wrapping paper,

and

Colouring-in

egg boxes,

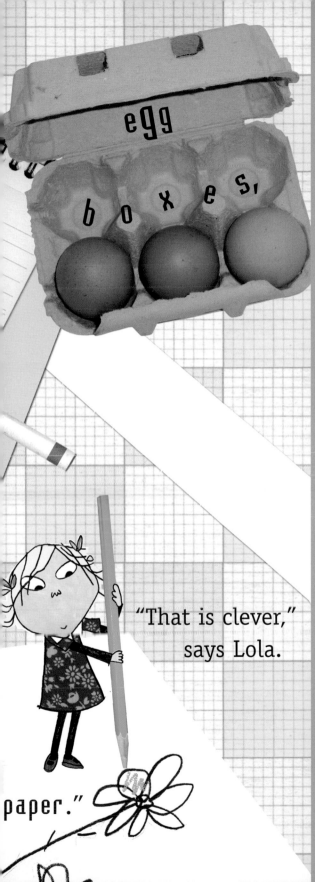

"That is clever," says Lola.

paper."

Later Lola says,
"Look, Charlie!
Mum bought me this special comic.
It's called

Look after YOUR Planet

and there's lots about recycling in it."

And I say, "Ooh! A **competition**. You can win a **tree** all of your own to plant."

"What do we have to do?" says Lola.

"We have to collect a hundred of each thing.

One hundred tin cans,

one hundred plastic things

and one hundred things made out of paper."

"That's a lot of things," says Lola.

"Look, Lola! Your very own tree counter."

"Every time you collect
something to **recycle**
you can stick a leaf
on to a branch.
When your **tree counter**
is completely full up
you can get your very own
real tree to plant."

Lola says,
"I would love to plant a **tree**."

"Well, you'd better
start **recycling**."

And Lola says,
"OK, Charlie!

This
box

is for

all the

plastic

things

and
this
one
is for
tin
cans

and
this
one
is for
paper.

And I have
already recycled
two plastic
things,
a baked bean tin,
and some paper."

I say, "I'm not sure we will be able to collect a hundred of each thing in just two weeks, Lola, all on our own."

And Lola says, "Of course we can, Charlie. Have you finished? Good..."

Later Lola says,
"See, Charlie! I can recycle these toilet rolls."

And I say, "The idea is to use the
paper really slowly and not waste it –
so we don't have to cut down lots of trees!
Then you recycle the rolls."

"Well, we need some more leaves on our tree counter. So maybe we need to ask some even more people."

The next day at school,
Lola says,
"We have to save the trees and stop
us being covered in a big
large pile of
rubbish.

If we fill this tree with leaves, we will win our very own real tree for the school."

Everyone is excited and says,

"I want to do recycling... pass it on."

"I want to do recycling... pass it on."

"I want to do recycling... pass it on."

So everyone at school starts **recycling**.

"Look how many I've got!"

"I've got lots too!"

"You are a **very** good recycler, Lotta!"

"Oh, Morten, you're not helping."

So Morten goes home...

... and he finds more things to **recycle**.

When everything is recycled,
Lola says,
"Oh no. We have NOT
filled up the
whole tree...
so we will NOT be
getting our
own real tree."

But then Morten
comes along.

Lotta says,

"**Look** at
what he's
GOT!"

And soon...

... we have **filled up** the **tree counter.**

"Thank you, Morten!" says Lola. "You are a very good recycler."

Then Marv whispers to Morten,
"Where did you get all that?"

And Morten says,
"Marty's bedroom."

Marv says,
"You are going
to be in

SUCH

big

trouble."

The next day we all go
    outside to plant our real,
actual school **tree**.

"Look! Our very own real school tree!" says Lola.
"We are extremely very good
recyclers, aren't we!"

Later, when we are all
round at Marv's, suddenly we hear,

"Who's been in my ROOM?"

"Let's get out of here!" says Marv.
And Morten says,
"Quick! Run for it!"